George Peele's The Battle of Alcazar: A Retelling

David Bruce

Published by David Bruce, 2022.

This is a work of fiction. Similarities to real people, places, or events are entirely coincidental.

GEORGE PEELE'S THE BATTLE OF ALCAZAR: A RETELLING

First edition. July 20, 2022.

Copyright © 2022 David Bruce.

ISBN: 979-8201592165

Written by David Bruce.

Table of Contents

Dedication

Dedicated to Carl Eugene Bruce and Josephine Saturday Bruce

My father, Carl Eugene Bruce, died on 24 October 2013. He used to work for Ohio Power, and at one time, his job was to shut off the electricity of people who had not paid their bills. He sometimes would find a home with an impoverished mother and some children. Instead of shutting off their electricity, he would tell the mother that she needed to pay her bill or soon her electricity would be shut off. He would write on a form that no one was home when he stopped by because if no one was home he did not have to shut off their electricity.

The best good deed that anyone ever did for my father occurred after a storm that knocked down many power lines. He and other linemen worked long hours and got wet and cold. Their feet were freezing because water got into their boots and soaked their socks. Fortunately, a kind woman gave my father and the other linemen dry socks to wear.

My mother, Josephine Saturday Bruce, died on 14 June 2003. She used to work at a store that sold clothing. One day, an impoverished mother with a baby clothed in rags walked into the store and started shoplifting in an interesting way: The mother took the rags off her baby and dressed the infant in new clothing. My mother knew that this mother could not afford to buy the clothing, but she helped the mother dress her baby and then she watched as the mother walked out of the store without paying.

My mother and my father both died at 7:40 p.m.

Educate Yourself

Read Like A Wolf Eats

Be Excellent to Each Other

Books Then, Books Now, Books Forever

In this retelling, as in all my retellings, I have tried to make the work of literature accessible to modern readers who may lack the knowledge about mythology, religion, and history that the literary work's contemporary audience had.

Do you know a language other than English? If you do, I give you permission to translate this book, copyright your translation, publish or self-publish it, and keep all the royalties for yourself. (Do give me credit, of course, for the original retelling.)

I would like to see my retellings of classic literature used in schools, so I give permission to the country of Finland (and all other countries) to give copies of this book to all students forever. I also give permission to the state of Texas (and all other states) to give copies of this book to all students forever. I also give permission to all teachers to give copies of this book to all students forever.

Teachers need not actually teach my retellings. Teachers are welcome to give students copies of my eBooks as background material. For example, if they are teaching Homer's *Iliad* and *Odyssey*, teachers are welcome to give students copies of my *Virgil's Aeneid: A Retelling in Prose* and tell students, "Here's another ancient epic you may want to read in your spare time."

CAST OF CHARACTERS

THE USURPER AND HIS SUPPORTERS:
The Moor Muly Mahamet.
Muly Mahamet, his son. Called Muly, Junior in this book.
Calipolis, wife of the Moor.
Pisano, a Captain of the Moor.
THE RIGHTFUL RULER AND HIS SUPPORTERS:
Abdelmelec, uncle of the Moor Muly Mahamet, and rightful ruler of
Morocco.
Mahamet Seth, younger brother of Abdelmelec.
Rubin Archis, widow of Abdelmunen, older brother of Abdelmelec.
Son of Rubin Archis.
Celybin, a follower of Abdelmelec.
Zareo, a follower of Abdelmelec.
Calsepius Bassa, a Turkish Captain.
Abdil Rayes, a Queen.
THE PORTUGUESE:
Sebastian, King of Portugal.
Duke of Avero, a follower of Sebastian.
Duke of Barceles, a follower of Sebastian.
Lord Lodowick, a follower of Sebastian.
Lewes de Silva, a follower of Sebastian.
Christophero de Tavera, a follower of Sebastian.
Don Diego Lopez, Governor of Lisbon.
Don de Menysis, Governor of Tangier.
Other Christians:
Tom Stukeley, Captain of the Papal fleet.
Irish Bishop.
Hercules, an Italian in Stukeley's service.
Jonas, an Italian in Stukeley's service.
APPEARING IN THE DUMB SHOWS:

The Presenter.

Abdelmunen, oldest brother of Abdelmelec.

Two young Brothers of the Moor Muly Mahamet.

Two Murderers.

Fame.

OTHER CHARACTERS:

Moorish Ambassadors, Spanish Ambassadors and Legate, Boy, Soldiers, Messengers, etc.

A *Queen.*

Ladies.

NOTES

• Sebastian was King of Portugal from 11 June 1557 to 4 August 1578. He was born on 20 January 1554.

• King Philip II of Spain reigned from 16 January 1556 to 13 September 1598.

• King Sebastian of Portugal and King Philip II of France were related. Charles V, Holy Roman Emperor, was the father of King Philip II and the grandfather of King Sebastian.

• In 1578 Portugal's King Sebastian invaded Morocco. The invasion ended in a disastrous defeat for Portugal.

• The Battle of Alcazar took place on 4 August 1578.

• George Peele makes the elder Muly Mahamet, who is ruling Morocco at the beginning of the play, a villain.

• George Peele regards Abdelmelec, an uncle to the Moor Muly Mahamet, as the rightful ruler of Morocco.

• The events of the play begin in 1576. Abdelmelec has re-entered Morocco in an attempt to take the crown away from the Moor Muly Mahamet. Abdelmelec has brought a large Turkish contingent with him.

• The rulers of Morocco had the title of "Muly." The title also was given to other male members of the royal family.

• "Bassa" is an early form of "Pasha," a title that Turkish military commanders often held.

• Barbary is North Africa west of Egypt, but often George Peele's characters use it to mean Morocco.

• Genealogy and History:

Muly Xarif, an immigrant from Arabia, became the ruler of Morocco.

Muly Xeque, the son of Muly Xarif, succeeded him.

Muly Xeque had four sons. The eldest — the Moor Muly Abdallas — succeeded him.

When Muly Abdallas died, his three brothers were supposed to succeed him, in order of age: Abdelmunen was the next oldest, followed by Abdelmelec and then Mahamet Seth (the youngest).

Muly Abdallas, however, reneged on his promise and put his own eldest son (the Moor Muly Mahamet) on the throne beside him.

In 1574 Abdallas died and Muly Mahamet became sole ruler of Morocco, although Abdallas' brothers had a better claim to the throne.

As the play opens, Abdelmunen is dead, and Abdelmelec is attempting to become the ruler of Morocco. In fact, he is the rightful ruler.

• Dumb shows are brief pantomimed scenes. They are the scenes the author of this book asks you to imagine in the prologue of each chapter.

• In the rhetorical device known as apostrophe, the speaker directly addresses a person who is not present.

• In Elizabethan culture, a man of higher rank would use words such as "thee," "thy," "thine," and "thou" to refer to a servant. However, two close friends or a husband and wife could properly use "thee," "thy," "thine," and "thou" to refer to each other.

• An excellent annotated edition of George Peele's play can be read and/or downloaded free at elizabethandrama.org:

https://tinyurl.com/rpczdc3

It is copyrighted by Peter Lukacs. If he had not written his annotated edition, I would not have written this retelling of the play.

CHAPTER 1

The Presenter says this to you, the audience:

"Honor, which is the spur that pricks the princely mind to follow rule and climb the stately chair that is the throne, with great desire inflames Sebastian, the young King of Portugal, an honorable and courageous king, to undertake a dangerous, dreadful war, and aid with Christian arms the barbarous Moor, the dark-skinned Muly Mahamet, who withholds the kingdom from his uncle Abdelmelec, whom proud Abdallas wronged, and in his throne installs his cruel son, who now usurps the position of this prince, this brave lord from Barbary: Muly Abdelmelec of Morocco."

In other words, this play will be about King Sebastian of Portugal fighting on the side of the Moor Muly Mahamet, a usurper of the throne of Morocco, against the rightful King of Morocco: Muly Abdelmelec.

The Presenter continued:

"The passage to the crown was made by murder.

"Abdallas died, and granted power to this tyrant king — Muly Mahamet — whose story we will relate — sprung from the Arabian Moor, black in his look, and bloody in his deeds. And in his shirt, stained with a cloud of gore, he presented himself, with naked sword in hand, accompanied, as now you may behold, with devils coated in the shapes of men."

Imagine this:

The Moor Muly Mahamet, his son, the Moor's attendant, and some pages who attend Muly Mahamet stand together. The Moor Muly Mahamet's two younger brothers arrive. Muly Mahamet shows them the bed, and then he and the others leave them, and they begin to sleep.

The Presenter continued:

"Some people are silenced by being murdered by kindred. Read onward and see what heinous stratagems these damned people contrive.

"Look, alas, this traitor-king sends these young lords, both of whom are his younger brothers, to their longest home — the grave — much like poor lambs prepared for sacrifice!"

Imagine this scene:

The Moor Muly Mahamet and two murderers bring into the bedroom his uncle Abdelmunen.

The two murderers then draw aside the curtains surrounding the bed and smother the two young princes in the bed.

After doing this in sight of Muly Mahamet's shocked uncle — Abdelmunen — the two murderers strangle him in his chair, and then go forth.

In other words, the Moor Muly Mahamet murders some of his relatives to keep his throne safe. He murders his younger brothers in case they later become ambitious, and he murders his uncle Abdelmunen, who in fact should have become the ruler of Morocco after Muly Mahamet's father died. Abdelmunen was naïve when he went with the Moor Muly Mahamet and two murderers into the bedroom.

Two other uncles are still alive who have a better claim to the throne than Muly Mahamet. This is the reason why:

Muly Xarif, an immigrant from Arabia, became the ruler of Morocco.

Muly Xeque, the son of Muly Xarif, succeeded him.

Muly Xeque had four sons. The eldest — the Moor Muly Abdallas — succeeded him.

When Muly Abdallas died, his three brothers — by a previous agreement — were supposed to succeed him, in order of age: Abdelmunen was the next oldest, followed by Abdelmelec and then Mahamet Seth (the youngest).

Muly Abdallas, however, reneged on his promise and put his own eldest son (the Moor Muly Mahamet) on the throne beside him.

In 1574 Abdallas died and Muly Mahamet became sole ruler of Morocco, although Abdallas' brothers had a better claim to the throne.

Muly Mahamet then murdered his two younger brothers and his uncle Abdelmunen.

The Presenter continued:

"Once his younger brothers were in the fatal bed behearsed, the dark-skinned Muly Mahamet put to death by proud command his father's brother, who innocently felt that he was safe with him.

"Don't say that these things are feigned, for they are true.

"Do understand how, eager to enjoy his father's crown, this unbelieving — non-Christian — Moor, murdering his uncle and his younger brothers, triumphs in his ambitious tyranny, until the goddess Nemesis, high mistress of revenge, who with her whip keeps all the world in awe, with thundering drums awakens the god of war, and calls the monstrous Furies — goddesses who punish those who murder relatives — from the steep rocks of Lake Avernus, located at one of the entrances of Hell, to wander and rage, and to inflict vengeance on this accursed Moor because of his sin.

"And now behold how Abdelmelec, the rightful ruler of Morocco and living uncle to this unhappy traitor-king, comes armed with the great aid that Amurath — Great Amurath, Turkish Emperor of the East — had sent for service done to Sultan Suleiman, under whose colors he had served in the battlefield.

"Abdelmelec had rendered this service after fleeing the fury of the dark-skinned Muly Mahamet's father, who had wronged his brothers and broken his agreement with them in order to install his son."

Muly Mahamet's father was Muly Abdallas, who had made Muly Mahamet his heir to the throne instead of the oldest of Muly Abdallas' brothers — Abdelmunen — as had been previously agreed.

The second oldest of Muly Abdallas' brothers — Abdelmelec — had fled and served the Sultan of the Ottoman Empire. He had served in the army of Selim II, the son of Sultan Suleiman.

Amurath, known now in history as Murad III, the son of Selim II, then aided Abdelmelec in his attempt to become the Muly of Morocco by giving him troops of soldiers.

The Presenter continued:

"Read on, and see this true and tragic war, a modern matter full of blood and sorrow, where three bold kings, confounded in their height, fell to the earth, contending for a crown.

"Call this war *the Battle of Alcazar*."

— 1.1 —

On the frontier between Morocco and Algeria, military drums and trumpets sounded, and then Abdelmelec, the Turkish captain Calsepius Bassa and his guards, and a Moor named Argerd Zareo stood together, along with some soldiers.

Abdelmelec was the rightful ruler of Morocco and was invading the country to take his rightful crown. Calsepius Bassa was the leader of the Turkish troops sent to support Abdelmelec. Argerd Zareo was a follower of Abdelmelec.

They had just arrived at the border of Morocco.

Abdelmelec said, "All hail, Argerd Zareo, and, you Moors, salute the frontiers of your native home."

Referring to himself in the third person, he continued:

"Cease, rattling drums; and, Abdelmelec, here throw up thy trembling hands to heaven's throne. Pay to thy God due thanks, and pay thanks to him who strengthens thee with mighty gracious arms against the haughty, arrogant usurper of thy right, the royal seat and crown of Barbary, Great Amurath, the great Emperor of the East.

"Let the world bear witness how I adore the sacred name of Amurath the Great.

"Calsepius Bassa, Bassa Calsepius, to thee, and to thy trusty band of men who carefully attend us in our camp, picked soldiers, comparable to the guard of Myrmidons who guarded Achilles' tent, such thanks we give to thee and to them all, as may concern a poor distressed king, in honor and in princely courtesy."

Achilles, the leader of the Myrmidons, was the greatest warrior in the Trojan War; he fought on the side of the Greeks against the Trojans.

Calsepius Bassa replied, "Courteous and honorable Abdelmelec, we have not come at the Ottoman Emperor Amurath's command as mercenary men to serve for pay, but as sure friends, by our great master sent to gratify and to remunerate thy love, thy loyalty, and thy eagerness, as well as thy service in his father's dangerous war, and to perform, in view of all the world, the true office of right and royalty.

"To see thee in thy kingly chair enthroned, to settle and to seat thee in the same, and to make thee Emperor of this Barbary are the reason the viceroys and sturdy janizaries of Amurath, grandson to Sultan Suleiman, have come here with thee."

Viceroys governed lands conquered by the Turkish Emperors. Janizaries are elite Turkish soldiers.

Mahamet Seth, Rubin Archis, Abdil Rayes, and others arrived.

Mahamet Seth was Abdelmelec's younger brother. Rubin Archis was the widow of Abdelmelec's older brother, Abdelmunen, who was murdered by Muly Mahamet, the usurping King of Morocco. Abdil Rayes was a Queen.

Abdil Rayes said, "Long live my lord, the sovereign of my heart, Lord Abdelmelec, whom the God of kings has made fortunate! And may Amurath live long for this good deed!"

Seth said, "Our Moors have seen the silver moons wave in banners bravely spreading over the plain, and in these semicircles have descried, all in a golden field, a star to rise, a glorious comet that begins to blaze, promising a happy and fortunate outcome to us all."

The silver moons were on the many banners of the Turkish soldiers.

In this society, astronomical events were thought to be omens, which could be either good or bad.

Rubin Archis, Abdelmunen's widow, said to Calsepius Bassa, "Brave man-at-arms, whom Amurath has sent to sow the lawful true-succeeding seed in Barbary, which bows and groans under a proud usurping tyrant's mace, right thou the wrongs this rightful king — Abdelmelec — has endured."

Abdelmelec said, "Distressed ladies, and you dames of Fez, capital city of Morocco, you who are descended from the true Arabian Muly Xarif, my grandfather and the loadstar and the honor of our line, now clear your watery eyes, wipe your tears away, and cheerfully give welcome to these soldiers, my army of Moroccan and Turkish troops.

"Amurath has sent scourges by his men to whip that tyrant traitor-king away from here — Muly Mahamet, who has usurped the throne from us, and maimed you all."

Abdelmelec then addressed his troops:

"Soldiers, since troops who fight on the rightful side of quarrels are successful, and since the men who manage them don't fight in fear as traitors and their feres — that is, their companions — so that you may understand what arms we bear, what lawful arms against our brother's son, the usurper, in the sight of heaven, even of my honor's worth, truly I will deliver and discourse the sum of my family history."

Using the royal plural, he said:

"Descended from the line of Mahomet, Muly Xarif — our grandfather — with much gold and treasure left Arabia and strongly planted himself in Barbary.

"Of the Moors who now metaphorically travel with us, our grandfather Muly Xarif was the first.

"From him, as well you know, was descended Muly Mahamet Xeque, our father, who in his lifetime made a perfect law, confirmed with the general voice of all his peers, that in his kingdom his sons should successively succeed.

"Abdallas was the first, the oldest of four.

"Abdelmunen was the second oldest.

"I was next oldest, and my brother Seth was youngest of all.

"Abdallas reigned for the rest of his life, but see the deviation he made from the agreement! He labored to invest his son — the Moor Muly Mahamet — in all, usurping the crown to disannul the law our father made and to disinherit us his brethren.

"And in his lifetime Abdallas wrongfully proclaimed his son to be king — his son Muly Mahamet who now contends with us.

"Therefore I crave to re-obtain my right that Muly Mahamet the traitor holds. He is traitor and bloody tyrant both at once, and he is the man who murdered both of his younger brothers.

"But on this damned wretch, this traitor-king, the gods shall pour down showers of sharp revenge.

"And thus to you a genealogy and history not to you unknown I have delivered, yet I did this for no distrust of loyalty, my well-beloved friends. Instead, I did it because keeping the reasons of these troubles fresh in your memory may so move your minds that you don't think your lives or honors too dear to be spent in just and honorable battle to establish the lawful true-succeeding prince on his rightful throne."

Calsepius Bassa said, "Just and honorable and no other than just and honorable we repute the cause that we eagerly undertake for thee, thrice-puissant and renowned Abdelmelec, and for thine honor, safety, and crown, we will unconditionally expose our lives and honors to all the dangers that attend our war. We all will do this as freely and as resolutely as any Moor whom thou most command."

Seth said, "And why is my brother Abdelmelec, then, so slow to chastise Muly Mahamet with the fury of the sword? Muly Mahamet's pride swells as he attempts to exert power and influence beyond his reach. Follow his pride with thy fury of revenge."

Rubin Archis, a poet as well as a widow, said, "Of death, of blood, of vengeance, and deep revenge, shall Rubin Archis frame her tragic songs. In blood, in death, in murder, and in misdeed and wickedness, this heaven's malice did begin and end."

Abdelmelec said to her, "Rubin, these rites to Abdelmunen's ghost have by this time pierced their way into Pluto's grave below. Pluto, the god of the underworld, has learned of your husband's death.

"The bells of Pluto roundly ring revenge. The Furies and the fiends conspire with thee. War bids me draw my weapons for revenge of my deep wrongs and my dear brother's death."

The Furies are three immortal goddesses of vengeance who punish especially those who murder relatives.

Seth said, "Don't sheath your swords, you soldiers of Amurath, and don't sheath your swords, you Moors of Barbary, who fight in right of your anointed king, but follow to the gates of death and hell, pale death and hell, to entertain his soul.

"Follow, I say, to the burning hellish river of Phlegethon, this traitor-tyrant and his companies."

Calsepius Bassa said, "Heave up your swords against these stony strongholds, wherein these barbarous rebels are enclosed. The gods call for Abdelmelec to sit upon the throne of Barbary."

Abdil Rayes said, "Bassa, great thanks. You are the honor of the Turks."

She then said, "Go forward, brave lords, and go to this rightful war! How can this battle be anything but successful, when in us courage meets with a rightful cause?"

Rubin Archis said, "Go in good time, my best-beloved lord, and be successful in thy work thou undertake!"

— 1.2 —

The Moor Muly Mahamet, Calipolis (his wife), and their son rode their chariot into a valley north of Fez. Moorish attendants walked on each side of the chariot. Pisano, who was Muly Mahamet's captain, was present with the Moor Muly Mahamet's guards and his treasure.

Muly Mahamet ordered, "Pisano, take a company of our cavalry with an equal number of light-armed cavalry and soldiers armed with pikes, and with our treasure-laden wagon march away before us by the valley of Scyras and those plots of ground that lead the lower way to the city of Moroccus. Our enemies keep upon the mountain-tops, and they have encamped themselves not far from Fez."

He and his troops were trying to escape from the nearby troops of Abdelmelec.

Muly Mahamet then said to his wife, Caliopolis, "Madam, gold is the glue, tendons, and strength of war, and we must see that our treasure may be transported safely."

He then ordered the people who would guard the wagon, "Leave!"

Pisano exited with the treasure-laden wagon of treasure and some of the guards.

Muly Mahamet then asked his son, "Now, boy, what's the news?"

Muly, Junior replied, "The news, my lord, is war, war and revenge, and, if I shall declare the details, things stay like this:

"Rubin, my great-uncle's wife, who wrings her hands because of Abdelmunen's death, accompanied with many high-ranking women of Fez in mourning clothes, near to Algiers encountered Abdelmelec, who directs his army, puffed up with Amurath's aid, against your strongholds and castles of defense.

"The younger brother, Mahamet Seth, greets the great Calsepius Bassa, whom the King of Turks sends to invade your right and royal realm, and he basely begs all these arch-rebels to inflict revenge upon our family."

Muly Mahamet said, "Why, boy, is Amurath's Bassa such a bug-bear that he is marked to do this doughty deed?"

He then pretended to address Calsepius Bassa:

"Then, Bassa, lock the winds in prisons made of brass, send thunder from heaven, damn wretched men to death, and take on thyself all the offices of Saturn's sons — the Olympian gods."

The gods meant were Pluto, god of the underworld; Neptune, god of the sea; and Jupiter (Jove), who dispensed justice on the earth.

"Be Pluto, then, in hell, and bar the fiends, take Neptune's force to thee and calm the seas, and execute Jove's justice on the world.

"Convey Tamburlaine into our Africa here to chastise and to menace lawful kings."

Tamburlaine was a bloodthirsty conqueror.

The Moor Muly Mahamet then pretended to address Tamburlaine, by whom he mockingly meant Calsepius Bassa:

"Tamburlaine, don't triumph, for thou must die, as Philip, Caesar, and Caesar's peers did."

Philip was the father of Alexander the Great, another conqueror. Julius Caesar and many of his peers also fought wars, including civil wars.

Muly, Junior then mentioned some things that had occurred in Abdelmelec's camp:

"The Bassa was grossly flattered to his face.

"Amurath's praise was advanced above the sound upon the plains.

"The soldiers were spread out on the land, as were that brave guard of sturdy janizaries that Amurath had given to Abdelmelec.

"With this gift of soldiers, Amurath bade Abdelmelec to boldly be with them as safe as if he slept within a walled town whose citizens had taken themselves to their weapons, threatening revenge, bloody revenge, bloody revengeful war against you."

The Moor Muly Mahamet said, "Leave, and let me hear no more of this.

"Why, boy, are we successor to the great Abdallas who descended from the Arabian Muly Xarif, and shall we be afraid of Bassas and of bug-bears that are raw-headed and bloody-boned?

"Boy, do thou see here this scimitar by my side?

"Since they begin to bathe in blood, let blood be the theme whereon our time shall tread. I shall make such slaughter with my weapon as our Moors shall sail in ships and pinnaces through the stream and deep bloody channels from the shore of Tangier to the gates of Fez."

Pinnaces are small ships that often serve as messenger-ships between larger ships.

Muly, Junior replied, "And of those slaughtered bodies I thy son shall erect a huge tower like Nimrod's frame to threaten those unjust and partial gods that to Abdallas' lawful seed deny a long, happy, and triumphant reign."

According to the Bible, Nimrod had attempted but failed to build a tower — the tower of Babel — that would reach heaven.

An alarm sounded, and a messenger entered.

The messenger said, "Flee, King of Fez, King of Moroccus, flee. Flee with thy friends, Emperor of Barbary. Oh, flee the sword and fury of the foes who rage as the lioness rages who rears up on her hind legs to rescue her younglings from the bear!

"Thy towns and holds by numbers basely yield and basely resign thy land to Abdelmelec's rule.

"Amurath's soldiers have captured thy wagon and thy treasure, and they have sworn thy death.

"Flee Amurath's army and Abdelmelec's threats, or thou and those with thee look to breathe your and their last here."

Muly Mahamet said, "Villain, what dreadful sound of death and flight is this with which thou afflict our ears?

"But if there is no safety to abide the favor, fortune, and success of war, let's leave in haste!

"Roll on, my chariot-wheels, restless until I am safely set in the shade of some unhaunted place, some blasted, blighted grove of deadly, poisonous yew or dismal cypress-tree, far from the light or comfort of the sun, there to curse heaven and he — and He — who heaves me away from here, and to sicken as if Envy were at Cecrops' gate, and to pine with thoughts and terror of mishaps."

The goddess Envy paid a visit to Cecrops' gate and made Aglauros, one of Cecrops' daughters, envious of her sister, whom the god Mercury loved. Aglauros attempted to keep Mercury from seeing her sister, and Mercury turned Aglauros into a stone statue.

The Moor Muly Mahamet thought that he would sicken with envy at the good fortune of Abdelmelec, and he would waste away with terrifying thoughts about the misfortunes that had and could happen to himself.

The Moor Muly Mahamet then said, "Let's leave!"

CHAPTER 2

— Prologue —

A call to arms sounded in the distance, and the Presenter appeared and said, "Now war begins its raging and ruthless reign, and Nemesis, with bloody whip in hand, thunders for vengeance on this dark-skinned Moor Muly Mahamet."

Imagine this:

Nemesis, the goddess of vengeance, appears. Then three ghosts appear.

The three ghosts were those of the three relatives Muly Mahamet had murdered: his two younger brothers and his uncle Abdelmunen.

The Presenter continued:

"Nor may the silence of the speechless, quiet night — night that is the dire architect of murders and misdeeds, of tragedies and tragic tyrannies — hide or contain this barbarous cruelty of this usurper to his progeny."

Imagine this:

The three ghosts cry, "Vindicta! Revenge!"

The Presenter continued:

"Listen closely, lords, to the dreadful shrieks and clamors that resound, as in a hollow place afar, and sound revenge upon this traitor's soul — the soul of this traitor to family and nature, to gods and men!

"Now Nemesis upon her echoing drum, moved with this ghastly moan, this sad complaint, sounds an alarm loudly into Alecto's ears, and with her thundering awakens her, where she and the other Furies, just imps of dire revenge, lie on beds of steel in a cave as dark as hell."

Imagine this:

The three Furies, one with a whip, another with a bloody torch, and the third with a chopping knife, arise. They are wearing steel armor.

The Presenter continued:

"'Revenge,' cries Abdelmunen's aggrieved ghost, and with the terror of this noise his ghost arouses these nymphs of Erebus."

Erebus is hell, and these nymphs of Erebus are the three Furies.

The Presenter continued:

"The souls of his unhappy brethren — the two murdered brothers of Muly Mahamet — ring out the words 'Avenge and revenge.'

"And now these torments of the world start up, awakened with the thunder of Rhamnusia's drum and fearful echoes of these aggrieved ghosts."

Rhamnusia is another name for the goddess Nemesis.

The Presenter mentioned the names of the three Furies:

"Alecto with her brand and bloody torch,

"Megaera with her whip and snaky hair,

"Tisiphone with her fatal murdering iron chopping knife.

"These three conspire, these three complain and moan."

In an apostrophe the Presenter addressed the absent Moor Muly Mahamet:

"Thus, Muly Mahamet, a council is held to avenge the wrongs and murders thou have done."

The Presenter then addressed you, the audience, and mentioned some events that followed the capture of the Moor Muly Mahamet's treasure-loaded wagon by Abdelmelec's forces.

"Imagine that by this time this barbarous Moor had lost his dignity and his diadem, and lives forlorn among the mountain-shrubs, and for his food he eats the flesh of savage beasts.

"Amurath's soldiers have by this time installed good Abdelmelec in his royal seat: the throne.

"The upper-class women of Fez and the ladies of the land, in honor of Amurath, the son of the Ottoman Sultan Suleiman the Magnificent, erect a statue made of beaten gold, and sing to Amurath songs of lasting praise.

"Muly Mahamet's fury has been overthrown, his cruelty controlled, and his pride rebuked."

The Presenter then explained what the Moor Muly Mahamet would do after he got over his depression following the loss of his kingdom:

"When sober thoughts will at last have renewed his concern for how to retake his kingdom and desired crown, he furiously will implore by messengers the aid from brave King Sebastian of Portugal that he once was offered and refused.

"King Sebastian, eager to engage in all arms and chivalry, will listen to the Moor Muly Mahamet's ambassadors, and will grant what they in letters and by words entreat.

"Now listen, lordings; now begins the game of Sebastian's tragedy in this tragic war."

— 2.1 —

Abdelmelec, Mahamet Seth, and Calsepius Bassa talked together on a battlefield near Fez. Some Moors and janizaries were present. Abdelmelec had just won a victory and become the ruler of Morocco.

Abdelmelec said, "Now the sun has displayed its golden beams, and now that the dusky clouds have dispersed, the sky clears and shows the twenty-colored rainbow.

"After this happy and fortunate fight, wherein our enemies have lost the day, and Victory, adorned with Fortune's plumes, alights on Abdelmelec's glorious crest, we find here time to catch our breath, and now begin to pay thy due and duties thou owe to heaven and earth, to gods and Amurath."

Abdelmelec used the royal plural in the first part of the last paragraph, but then he switched to "thy" and "thou" when referring to himself as a way of showing his respect to heaven and earth, to gods and Amurath.

Trumpets sounded.

Abdelmelec continued, "And now draw near, and let heaven and earth give ear, give ear and record, heaven and earth, with me.

"You lords of Barbary, listen and pay attention, pay close attention to the words I speak and the vow I make to plant the true succession of the crown.

"Lo, lords, we install our only brother here in our royal seat to succeed me, and by the name of Mahamet Seth entitle him true heir to the crown. Seth will become King of Morocco after I die.

"May you gods of heaven congratulate this deed, so that men on earth may therewith stand content!

"Lo, thus I pay my due and duties to heaven and earth, to gods and Amurath!"

Trumpets sounded.

Seth said to Calsepius Bassa, "Renowned Bassa, to remunerate thy worthiness and magnanimity, behold, the noblest ladies of the land bring to you tokens of their gratitude."

Rubin Archis, her son, the queen Abdil Rayes, and some ladies walked over to him.

Rubin Archis, the widow of Abdelmunen, said, "Rubin, who lives only for revenge, by this gift commends herself to thee, Bassa. Receive the token of her thankfulness. To Amurath the god of earthly kings, Rubin gives and sacrifices her son. Not with sweet smoke of fire or sweet perfume, but with his father's sword and his mother's thanks, Rubin gives her son to Amurath."

Her son will serve Amurath.

Abdil Rayes, who was a queen and used the royal plural, said, "As Rubin gives her son, so we give ourselves to Amurath and fall before his face."

She prostrated herself and then stood.

She gave some gold jewelry to Calsepius Bassa as she said, "Bassa, wear thou the gold of Barbary, and glisten like the palace of the Sun, in honor of the deed that thou have done."

Calsepius Bassa said, "Well worthy of the aid of Amurath are Abdelmelec and these noble dames."

He said to Rubin Archis, "Rubin, thy son I shall before long bestow, where thou bequeath him in honor's fee, on Amurath the mighty Emperor of the East, who shall receive the scion of your royal family with cheerful looks and gleams of princely grace."

He then said to Abdelmelec, "This chosen guard of Amurath's janizaries I leave to honor and attend on thee, King of Morocco, conqueror of thy foes, true King of Fez, Emperor of Barbary.

"Muly Abdelmelec, live and keep thy seat, in spite of fortune's spite or enemies' threats."

Referring to himself, Calsepius Bassa said, "Ride, Bassa, now, bold Bassa, homeward ride, as glorious as great Pompey in his pride."

Calsepius Bassa now left to return home to serve Amurath.

Pompey was a Roman general who died in one of Rome's civil wars.

— 2.2 —

Don Diego Lopez, the Irish Bishop, the Englishman Stukeley, Hercules, Jonas, and others stood together in Lisbon, the capital of Portugal.

Don Diego Lopez was the governor of Lisbon, and he was greeting these men who had sailed their ship into Lisbon's port.

Stukeley was the English commander of the forces on the ship. Hercules and Jonas were Italian soldiers serving Stukeley. Hercules was Stukeley's second-in-command.

Don Diego Lopez said, "Welcome to Lisbon, valiant Catholics. Welcome, brave Englishmen, to Portugal.

"Most reverend primate of the Irish church, and, noble Stukeley, famous by thy name, welcome, thrice welcome to King Sebastian's town."

A primate in Catholicism is a high-ranking priest: a chief bishop or archbishop.

Don Diego Lopez continued, "And welcome, English captains, to you all."

Don Diego Lopez knew that Stukeley was English, and so he assumed that Hercules and Jonas were English, but they were Italian.

He continued, "It makes us joyous to see his Holiness' fleet cast anchor happily upon our coast."

The Irish bishop replied, "These welcomes, worthy governor of Lisbon, are evidence of an honorable mind in thee, but be aware of our misfortune also."

Don Diego Lopez had assumed that their ships had intentionally arrived in Lisbon, but actually bad weather had forced their ships to land there.

The Irish bishop continued, "We were all bound to Ireland by Pope Gregory's command, and therefore we embarked to land our forces there with the Irish unaware, conquering the island for his Holiness, and so restore it to the Roman faith.

"This was the reason of our expedition, and Ireland long before this would have been subdued, had not foul weather brought us to this bay."

Don Diego Lopez said, "Correct me if I'm wrong, but aren't you all Englishmen, and doesn't Ireland belong to that kingdom, lords?

"If so, then may I speak my conscience in the cause without scandal to the Holy See of Rome that this expedition is dishonorable and it is unfitting for you to meddle in."

Stukeley said, "Lord governor of Lisbon, understand, as we Englishmen are Englishmen, so are we men.

"I am Stukeley, and I am so determined in all I do to strive for rule, honor, and power that I am not to be bent so strictly to the place wherein at first I blew the fire of life, but that instead I may at liberty make choice of all the continents that bound the world because I make it not so great desert to be begotten or born in any place, since that's a thing of pleasure and of ease that might have been performed elsewhere as well."

Although he was English, Stukeley was not patriotic; instead, he was out to gain power for himself.

Don Diego Lopez said, "Follow what your good pleasure will, good Captain Stukeley. Far be it from me to make objections beyond my privilege and what is proper."

The Irish bishop said, "Yet, Captain Stukeley, give me permission to speak. We must love our country as our parents, and if at any time we alienate our love or efforts from doing it honor, it must concern motives and touch the soul as a matter of conscience and religion, and not as a matter of desire of rule or benefit."

He was saying that he believed in patriotism, and he believed that if one were to go against one's country, it must be out of considerations of conscience and religion, and not out of concern for one's personal gain.

He himself wanted Ireland to be under the control of the Holy See because of his religion.

Stukeley said, "Well said, bishop! Spoken like yourself — the reverent, lordly Bishop of Saint Asses."

Hercules said, "The bishop talks according to his coat, and does not take the measure of it by his mind. You see he has thus made his coat large and wide because he may convert it, as he wishes, to any form that may fit the fashion best."

Like Stukeley, Hercules was suspicious of the Irish bishop. He was saying that the Irish bishop would always take the Pope's side and would say whatever would serve the Pope's interests.

The Irish bishop replied to Hercules, "Captain, you do me wrong to speak like this about my coat or double conscience, and cannot answer it in another place."

His double conscience was as a man and as a bishop. Hercules had accused him of giving up the autonomy that belonged to him as a man of free will in order to serve the Catholic Church.

To some extent, this is true. A religious vow such as that taken by a priest involves giving up some free will. A Catholic priest can no longer stay true to his vow of chastity and get married and have children. He has given up the free will needed to choose to get married and have children.

The Irish bishop was also saying that his religion forbade the fighting of duels. Hercules' words could very well make a non-priest challenge him.

In addition, Hercules' words could be used against him on the Day of Judgment.

Wanting to make peace, Don Diego Lopez said, "His talk is only in jest, lord bishop; set aside the argument and all as friends deign to be entertained as my ability here can make provision.

"Shortly I shall conduct you to King Sebastian of Portugal, whose welcomes to foreigners are always princely and honorable, as is fitting for his state."

Stukeley said, "Thanks, worthy governor."

He then said to the Irish bishop, "Come, bishop, come. Will you display the fruits of quarrel and of wrath? Come, let's go in with my Lord of Lisbon here and put all conscience into one carouse, letting it out again as we may live and choose."

Everyone except Stukeley exited.

Alone, Stukeley spoke about what was most valuable to him:

"No action shall pass my hand or sword that cannot make a step to gain a crown.

"No word shall pass the office of my tongue that sounds not of affection to a crown.

"No thought shall have existence in my lordly breast that works not every way to win a crown.

"All my deeds, words, and thoughts shall be as a king's.

"My chiefest company shall be with kings, and my rewards shall be equivalent to a king's.

"Why shouldn't I, then, look to be a king?

"I am now already called the Marquis of Ireland, and I will be shortly King of Ireland.

"I had rather be the king of a molehill than the richest subject of a monarchy.

"Swell with pride, my worthy mind, and never cease to aspire until thou reign sole king of thy desire."

— 2.3 —

The Moor Muly Mahamet, Calipolis (his wife), their son, and two other Moors who served them stood near each other in the mountains of northern Morocco.

Muly Mahamet asked rhetorically, "Where are thou, boy? Where is Calipolis?"

They were in a wild area, not in a luxurious palace.

He looked around at the wild area and said, "Oh, deadly wound that passes by my eye! Oh, fatal poison of my swelling heart!"

He paused and then mourned, "Oh, fortune constant in unconstancy!

"Fight earthquakes in the entrails of the earth, and eastern whirlwinds in the hellish shades! May some foul contagion of the infected heaven blast all the trees, and may the unpropitious night-raven and tragic owl in their cursed high places breed and become foretellers of my fall, the fatal ruin of my fame and me!"

The screeches of night-ravens and owls were bad omens.

Muly Mahamet continued, "May adders and serpents hiss at my disgrace, and wound the earth with anguish of their stings!"

He then addressed the absent Abdelmelec, who had replaced him as King of Morocco, "Now, Abdelmelec, now triumph in Fez; fortune has made thee King of Barbary."

Calipolis, his wife, said, "Alas, my lord, what use are these huge exclamations of pain to help us in this distressed estate?

"Oh, pity our distressed condition, my lord, and turn all curses to humble lamentations, and those lamentations to actions of relief!

"I faint from hunger, my lord; and cursing complaints cannot refresh the fading substance of my life."

Muly Mahamet said, "Let all the world faint, rot, and be accursed, since my power faints and is accursed."

Calipolis said, "Yet have patience, lord, so you can conquer sorrows."

In this society, wives called their husbands "lord."

Muly Mahamet said, "What patience is for him who lacks his crown? There is no patience where the loss is such. The shame of my disgrace has put on wings, and swiftly flies around this earthly ball.

"Do thou care to live, then, foolish Calipolis, when he who should give essence to thy soul, he on whose glory all thy joy should rest, is soul-less, glory-less, and desperate, crying for battle, famine, sword, and fire, rather than calling for relief or life?

"But be content, thy hunger shall have an end. Famine herself shall waste away to death, and thou shall live. I will go hunt in these cursed solitary lands, and make my sword and shield here my hounds to pull down lions and untamed beasts."

He exited to hunt food.

Muly, Junior said, "Tush, mother, cherish your disheartened soul and feed with hope of happiness and ease. For if by valor or by strategy my kingly father can be fortunate, we shall be Jove's commanders once again and flourish in a three-fold happiness."

One of the Moors with them said, "His majesty Muly Mahamet has sent Sebastian, the good and innocent King of Portugal, a promise to resign the royalty and kingdom of Morocco to his hands."

The Moor Muly Mahamet had promised to give much power in Morocco to King Sebastian of Portugal if he would help him defeat Abdelmelec.

Muly, Junior continued, "And when this lofty offer takes effect, and instills boldness in Sebastian, my gracious lord Muly Mahamet — warned wisely to think this over — I don't doubt but will watch for opportunity, and take her forelock by the slenderest hair, to rid us of this miserable life."

The Moor Muly Mahamet would likely take the opportunity to give King Sebastian much less power in Morocco than he had been promised.

Muly, Junior said, "Good madam, cheer yourself up. My father's wise. He can submit himself and live below his station, make a show of friendship, promise, vow, and swear, until, by the virtue of his fair pretense, Sebastian trusts his integrity, and my father makes himself possessor of such fruits as grow upon such great advantages."

Calipolis said, "But more dishonor hangs on such misdeeds than all the profit their return can bear. Such secret judgments have the heavens imposed upon the drooping state of Barbary, as public merits in such lewd attempts have drawn with violence upon our heads."

In order for the Moor Muly Mahamet to convince King Sebastian to help him overthrow Abdelmelec, he would make promises that he did not intend to keep. Such false promises, according to Calipolis, are punished by heaven.

The Moor Muly Mahamet returned with a piece of meat on the end of his sword.

He said, "Hold on, Calipolis. Eat, and faint no more. I forced a lioness to leave this meat. It is the meat of a princess, and it is for a princess meet."

The lioness is the female royalty of beasts.

The Moor Muly Mahamet continued, "Learn by her noble stomach to regard penury as plenty in the most extreme dearth."

As his next sentences would make clear, he meant this: Even when you are very impoverished, regard yourself as having plenty because you have the ability to go out and get what you need.

He continued, "The lioness, when she saw that she was bereft of her meat, did not waste away in melancholy or childish fear, but as brave minds are strongest in extremes, so she, redoubling her former force, ranged through the woods, and rent the breeding vaults — the dwellings — of proudest savages to save herself."

The lioness, once her meat was taken away by Muly Mahamet, did not sit and mourn, but instead went out and killed something proud and savage so she could eat.

He continued, "Eat, then, and don't faint, fair Calipolis. For rather than fierce famine prevailing to gnaw thy entrails with her thorny teeth, the conquering lioness shall be thy servant, and lay huge heaps of slaughtered carcasses as bulwarks in the way of famine, to keep famine away.

"I will provide thee with a princely osprey, which as she flies over fish in pools, shall charm the fish so that they shall turn their glistening bellies up to be captured, and thou shall take thy liberal choice of all the fish.

"Jove's stately bird — the eagle — with wide-commanding wings shall hover always about thy princely head and beat down fowl by shoals into thy lap so that thou can eat.

"Eat, then, and don't faint, fair Calipolis."

Calipolis said, "Thanks, my good lord, and although my stomach is too queasy to digest such bloody meat, yet I will strengthen my stomach by using the virtue of my mind. I doubt not a whit that I shall live, my lord."

The Moor Muly Mahamet said, "Go into the shade, then, fair Calipolis, and give thy son and the Moors here some food."

He then said to all present, "Eat and be fat, so that we may meet the foe with strength and terror, to revenge the wrong done to us."

— 2.4 —

King Sebastian, the Duke of Avero, the Duke of Barceles, Lewes de Silva, and Christophero de Tavera met together in a room in the Royal Palace in Lisbon, Portugal. Some attendants were present.

King Sebastian ordered, "Call forth those Moors, those ambassadors of Barbary, who came with letters from the King of Fez."

One of the attendants exited and then returned, bringing in the Moorish ambassadors with two Moorish attendants.

King Sebastian said, "You warlike lords, and men of chivalry, honorable ambassadors of this high regent, the Moor Muly Mahamet, listen to King Sebastian of Portugal.

"These letters sent from your distressed lord, who was torn from his throne by Abdelmelec's hand, which was strengthened and raised by furious Amurath, ask for a kingly favor from me: aid to re-obtain his royal seat and place his fortunes in their former height.

"For repayment of which honorable arms, by these letters of his he firmly vows wholly to yield and to surrender the kingdom of Morocco into our hands, and to become to us contributory and to content himself with the realm of Fez."

The Moor Muly Mahamet was promising to let King Sebastian be the overlord of Morocco, and he was promising to pay tribute to him. Muly Mahamet would govern the city of Fez.

King Sebastian continued, "These lines, my lords, written in extreme circumstances, extend therefore only during fortune's date. They apply only as long as he has bad fortune. How shall Sebastian, then, believe these lines?"

He believed it possible that Muly Mahamet would forget his promises once Abdelmelec had been defeated.

The first ambassador said, "Viceroys, and most Christian King of Portugal, to satisfy thy doubtful mind herein, command forthwith that a blazing brand of fire be brought into the presence of thy majesty. Then thou shall see, by our most inviolate religious vows and ceremonies, how firm our sovereign's promises are."

An attendant brought in a blazing firebrand.

The first ambassador continued, "Behold, my lord. This binds our faith to thee. In token that great Muly Mahamet's hand has written no more than his brave heart intends to fulfill, and that his hand has written no more than he will perform to thee and to thine heirs, we offer here our hands into this flame, and as this flame fastens on this flesh, so from our souls we wish it may consume the heart of our great lord and sovereign, Muly Mahamet, King of Barbary, if his intent does not agree with his words!"

Each of the Moorish ambassadors put a hand into the fire and let the fire burn it.

Using the royal plural, King Sebastian said, "These ceremonies and protestations persuade us, you lords of Barbary; therefore, return this answer to your king. Assure him by the honor of my crown, and by

Sebastian's true unfeigned faith, he shall have aid and succor to recover, and seat him in, his former dominion.

"Let him rely upon our princely word. Tell him that by August we will come to him with such an army of brave impatient minds that Abdelmelec and great Amurath shall tremble at the strength of Portugal."

The first ambassador said, "Thanks to the renowned King of Portugal, on whose bold promises our state depend."

King Sebastian said, "Men of Barbary, go and gladden your distressed king and say that Sebastian lives to right his wrong."

The ambassadors and their attendants exited.

King Sebastian ordered, "Duke of Avero, call in those Englishmen, Don Stukeley, and those captains of the fleet that recently landed in our bay of Lisbon."

He thought to himself, *Now breathe, Sebastian, and in breathing blow some gentle gale of thy new-formed joys.*

He was looking forward to leading a crusade in north Africa.

As the Duke of Avero was leaving, King Sebastian said, "Duke of Avero, it shall be your charge to take the muster of the Portuguese and the bravest bloods of all our country."

The Duke of Avero would have the responsibility of raising an army in Portugal.

The Duke of Avero exited.

King Sebastian then made more orders:

"Lewes de Silva, you shall be dispatched with letters to King Philip the Second of Spain. Tell him we crave his aid in this behalf. I know that our fellow-king Philip will not deny his futherance in this holy Christian war.

"Duke of Barceles, as thy ancestors have always been loyal to Portugal, so now, in honor of thy promising youth, thy charge shall be to go to Antwerp speedily, to hire us mercenary men-at-arms. Promise them princely pay; and be thou assured thy word is ours — Sebastian speaks the word."

King Sebastian would pay whatever the Duke of Barceles offered the mercenaries.

Christophero de Tavera requested, "I beseech your majesty to employ me in this war."

King Sebastian said, "Christopher de Tavera, you are next to myself, you are my good Hephaestion, and you are my bedfellow, and so thy cares and mine shall be alike in this, and thou and I will live and die together."

Hephaestion was Alexander the Great's closest friend.

In this society, unmarried people of the same sex often slept in the same bed without causing scandal.

The Duke of Avero returned, leading the Irish bishop, Stukeley, Jonas, Hercules, and others.

Like Don Diego Lopez before him, King Sebastian assumed that the newcomers were Englishmen.

He said, "And now, brave Englishmen, to you whom angry storms have forced you to put into our bay, don't regard your fortune as being any the worse in this. We hold our foreigners' honors in our hand, and we give the distressed frank and free relief.

"Tell me, then, Stukeley, for that's thy name, I believe, will thou, in honor of thy country's fame, risk thy person in this brave exploit, and follow us to fruitful Barbary, with these six thousand soldiers thou have brought, who were choicely picked from throughout wanton Italy?

"Thou are a man of gallant appearance, proud in thy looks, and famous in every way. Frankly tell me, will thou go with me?"

Stukeley replied, "Courageous king, you are the wonder of my thoughts, and yet, my lord, with pardon understand that I myself and these whom weather has forced to lie at anchor here by thy gracious coast have directed our course and are making full force straight for Ireland."

King Sebastian said, "For Ireland, Stukeley — thou make me wonder much — with seven ships, two pinnaces, and six thousand men?

"I tell thee, Stukeley, they are far too weak to violate the Queen of Ireland's right, for Ireland's Queen commands England's force."

The Queen of Ireland (and England) was Elizabeth I; in 1542, her father, Henry VIII, had been named King of Ireland.

King Sebastian continued, "Even if every ship were ten thousand on the seas, manned with the strength of all the eastern kings, conveying all the monarchs of the world, to invade the island where her highness reigns, it would all be in vain, for heavens and destinies attend and wait upon her majesty. Sacred, imperial, and holy is her seat, shining with wisdom, love, and mightiness.

"Nature that made everything imperfect, fortune that never yet was found to be constant, and time that defaces every golden show dare not decay, remove, or impair her. Nature, time, and fortune have all agreed to bless and serve her royal majesty.

"Surrounding her is the surging ocean, whose raging floods swallow up her foes and split their ships in pieces on the rocks, and even in Spain, where all the traitors dance and play upon a sunny day, the surging ocean waters securely guard the western part of her isle.

"The south of her isle is enclosed by the narrow Britain-sea, where Neptune sits in triumph to direct to hell all who aim at her disgrace.

"The German seas that run along her isle's east are where Venus feasts all her water-nymphs — Venus, who with her beauty glancing on the waves sullies by contrast the cheek of the fair goddess Proserpina.

"Think carefully, then, proud Stukeley, before thou go on to wrong Elizabeth — the wonder of the highest God — since danger, death, and hell will follow thee and all those who seek to endanger her.

"If honor is the target at which thou aim, then follow me in holy Christian wars, and cease to seek thy country's overthrow."

Stukeley said, "My lord, let me admire these words of yours rather than answer your firm objections.

"His Holiness Pope Gregory the Seventh [actually, the Thirteenth] has made us four the leaders of the rest. Among these leaders, my lord, I am only one.

"If they agree, Stukeley will be the first to die with honor for Sebastian."

King Sebastian said, "Tell me, lord bishop, captains, tell me, all of you, are you content to leave this enterprise against your country and your countrymen, and to instead aid King Mahamet of Barbary?"

The Irish bishop said, "To aid King Mahamet of Barbary is against our vows, great King Sebastian of Portugal."

"Then, captains, what do you say?" King Sebastian asked.

Jonas said, "I say, my lord, as the Irish bishop said, we may not turn from conquering Ireland."

Hercules said, "Our country and our countrymen will condemn us worthy of death, if we neglect our vows."

King Sebastian said, "Consider, lords, that you are now in Portugal, and I may now dispose of you and yours. Haven't the wind and weather given you up and made you captives subject to our royal will?"

"It has, my lord, and willingly we yield to be commanded by your majesty," Jonas said. "But if you make us men who act out of free will, our course is then set directly for Ireland."

Using the royal plural, King Sebastian replied, "That course we will direct for Barbary."

He then said, "Follow me, lords. Sebastian leads the way to plant the Christian faith in Africa."

Stukeley said to himself:

"Saint George for England! And Ireland now adieu,

"For here Tom Stukeley shapes his course anew."

CHAPTER 3

The Presenter said:

"Lo, thus the brave courageous King of Portugal has drenched himself in a lake of blood and gore, and now he prepares in full haste with sails and oars to cross the swelling seas, with men and ships, and with courage and cannon-shot, to set this cursed Moor in his fatal hour.

"And in this Catholic cause King Philip the Second of Spain is called upon by sweet Sebastian, who overindulging in the prime time of his youth on ambitious poison, dies thereon.

"By this time the Moor has come to Tangier, a city belonging to the Portuguese.

"And now the King of Spain promises with holy face, as favoring the honor of the cause, his aid of arms, and he swiftly levies men to serve as soldiers.

"But nothing less than King Sebastian's good, he intends; at Guadalupe he met, some say, in person with the King of Portugal, and he attempted to arrange a marriage of his daughter with King Sebastian.

"But beware ambitious wiles and poisoned eyes! There was neither aid of arms nor of marriage, for King Sebastian went on his way without those Spaniards."

Imagine this:

Nemesis, the goddess of vengeance, appears. The three Furies bring to Nemesis scales in which to weigh the guilt or innocence of some of the principal players in this historical event. The three Furies then bring in some of the principal players, including Stuckeley and the Moor Muly Mahamet.

— 3.1 —

King Sebastian, some lords, Lewes de Silva, and the ambassadors and the legate of Spain met together in the Royal Palace in Lisbon, Portugal. Lewes de Silva had just returned from Spain, where he had carried letters from King Sebastian asking for King Philip II's assistance in fighting a war in Morocco to make the Moor Muly Mahamet the King of Morocco again.

King Sebastian said, "Honorable lords, ambassadors of Spain, the many favors by our meetings done from our beloved and renowned fellow-king, Philip the Catholic King of Spain, tell us therefore, my good lord ambassador. Tell us how your mighty master is minded to propagate the fame of Portugal."

The first Spanish ambassador said, "To propagate the fame of Portugal and to plant the religious truth of Christianity in Africa, Philip the Second, the great and powerful King of Spain, for the love and honor of Sebastian's name, promises the aid of arms, and he swears by us to do your majesty all the good he can, with men, munitions, and supply of war, of proud Spanish soldiers, in King Sebastian's aid, to spill their blood in honor of their Christ."

The Spanish legate said, "And farther, to manifest to your majesty how much the Catholic King of Spain favors this war with Moors and Muslim men of little faith, the honor of your everlasting praise, behold, to honor and enlarge thy name, he offers his daughter Isabel to link in marriage with the brave Sebastian; and to enrich Isabel, Sebastian's noble wife, his majesty promises as her dowry to resign the titles of the Moluccas Islands, which are also known as the Spice Islands, that by his sovereignty in the west Indies he commands. King Philip vows to give to King Sebastian these favors with unfeigned love and zeal."

King Sebastian said, "And may God so deal with King Sebastian's soul as justly as King Sebastian intends to fight for Christ!

"Nobles of Spain, the strongholds our renowned fellow-king, Philip the king of honor and of zeal, offers to me by you the chosen orators and envoys of Spain are not so precious in our account as is the peerless dame whom we adore, his daughter, in whose loyalty consists the life and honor of Sebastian.

"As for the aid of arms he promises, we will expect and thankfully receive those arms at Cadiz, where we will stop as we sail along the coast."

King Sebastian said to himself, "Sebastian, clap thy hands for joy, honored by this meeting and this match."

He then said out loud, "Go, lords, and follow to the famous war your king; and may his fortune be in all such as he intends to command arms in right."

In other words, let King Philip II of Spain's luck and fortune be as good as his intentions.

Everyone except Stukeley and the Duke of Avero exited.

Stukeley said, "Sit fast, Sebastian, for by your so doing that, God and good men will labor for Portugal!"

Stukeley felt that the best thing for King Sebastian to do would be to stay at home in Portugal, for as he would next say, he didn't think that King Philip II of Spain would keep his promise to render aid to Sebastian's military expedition.

He continued, "For the King of Spain, lying with a double face, flatters thy youth and eagerness, good King Sebastian of Portugal."

He then addressed King Philip II in an apostrophe, "Philip, whom some call the Catholic king, I much fear that thy faith will not be firm, but will disagree with what thou have promised."

The Duke of Avero said, "What, then, shall become of those men of war, those numbers of Spanish soldiers who multiply in Spain?"

Both men were aware that King Philip II of Spain was raising an army.

Stukeley said, "The King of Spain has a use for them and their supplies.

"The Spaniard, who is himself ready to embark, here gathers to a head like a pus-filled boil ready to burst, but I fear all too surely that Flanders shall feel the force of Spain."

The Spanish soldiers would be used to fight a war in northern Europe rather than assisting King Sebastian in northern Africa.

Stukeley continued, "Let the King of Portugal fare as he may or can, for the King of Spain intends to expend no powder on the Moors."

The Duke of Avero said, "If kings do dally so with holy oaths, the heavens will right the wrongs that they sustain. The kings will be punished for so lightly disregarding the holy oaths that they have made."

He then addressed King Philip II in an apostrophe, "Philip, if these forgeries be in thee, assure thyself, king, it will light on thee at last.

"And when proud Spain hopes soundly to prevail,

"The time may come that thou and thine shall fail."

— 3.2 —

Abdelmelec, Mahamet Seth, and Zareo talked together in Fez, the capital city of Morocco. A train of attendants was present.

Using the royal plural, Abdelmelec said, "The King of Portugal, led with deceiving hope, has raised his army, and received our foe — the deposed Moor Muly Mahamet — with honorable welcomes and regard, and has left his country-bounds, and comes here to Morocco in the hope of helping Mahamet to a crown. The King of Portugal hopes to chase us away from here, and plant in our place this dark-skinned Moor, who clads himself in a coat of hammered steel armor to heave us from the honor we possess.

"But, because I myself have been a soldier, I have, in pity for the King of Portugal, sent secret messengers to counsel him."

King Sebastian of Portugal would disregard those messengers.

Abdelmelec continued, "As for the aid of the King of Spain, which the Portuguese hoped to obtain, we have dispatched our letters to their king, Philip the Second, to request that in a quarrel so unjust, he who is called the Catholic king would not assist a reckless Christian prince: Sebastian.

"And, as by letters we are let to know, our offer of the seven strongholds we made he thankfully receives with all conditions, differing in his mind as far from all his words and promises to King Sebastian as we would wish, or you, my lords, desire."

Just as Stukeley and the Duke of Avero had thought, King Philip II of Portugal would not keep his word to assist King Sebastian. Instead, he had accepted Abdelmelec's bribe.

Zareo said, "What remains to be done, then, but for Abdelmelec to beat back this proud invading King of Portugal, and chastise this ambitious dark-skinned Moor with a thousand deaths for a thousand damned deeds!"

Abdelmelec said, "Forward, Zareo, and all you manly Moors!"

In an apostrophe, he addressed the King of Portugal, "Sebastian, see in time about thyself: If thou and thine who are misled thrive amiss, guiltless is Abdelmelec of thy blood."

— 3.3 —

Don de Menysis, who was the Governor of Tangier, met with his captains in the Portuguese-held fortress at Tangier. Others were present.

Don de Menysis said, "Captains, we have received letters from King Sebastian ordering that with signs and evidence of respect and friendship we entertain the King of Barbary, the Moor Muly Mahamet, who marches toward Tangier with his men, the poor remainders of those who fled from Fez when Abdelmelec won the glorious day of battle and installed himself in his imperial throne."

The first captain said, "Lord governor, we are ready to welcome and receive this unfortunate king who has been chased from his land by angry Amurath, and if the right rests in this vigorous Moor, bearing an unvanquishable princely heart, a noble resolution then it is in brave Sebastian our Christian king to aid this Moor with his victorious arms, thereby to propagate religious truth and plant his springing praise of God in Africa."

The second captain said, "But when will this brave Sebastian arrive to unite his forces with this manly Moor, so that both in one, and one in both, may join in this attempt of noble consequence?

"Our men of Tangier long to see their king, whose princely face, like the summer's sun, gladdens all these closest parts of Barbary."

Don de Menysis said, "Captains, he comes toward here at full speed, using both top sail and top-gallant sail, all in brave array.

"On the twenty-sixth day of June, he left the bay of Lisbon, and with all his fleet he happily arrived at Cadiz in Spain on the eighth of July, waiting for the aid that King Philip the Second of Spain had promised.

"And for fifteen days he there remained aboard, waiting for when this Spanish force would come, nor did he step ashore, as if he were continually sailing on the sea.

"But the King of Spain, who meant and intended nothing less, pretended to experience a sudden fear and anxiety that necessitated him to keep his own country safe from Amurath's fierce invasion, and to excuse his promise to our king, for which he stormed as great Achilles did long ago while lying for lack of wind in Aulis' gulf."

Ancient Greek ships met at the gulf of Aulis before sailing to Troy. Achilles, the greatest warrior of the Trojan War, was impatient at the delay caused by lack of the wind needed to sail to Troy.

Don de Menysis continued, "And King Sebastian hoisted up his sails and weighed his anchors, and hitherward he came, and looked to meet this manly Moor whose cause he undertakes.

"Therefore we go to welcome and receive, with cannon-shot and shouts of young and old, this fleet of Portuguese and troop of Moors."

— 3.4 —

At the Portuguese-held city of Tangier, trumpets sounded, and small cannon discharged their cannon-shot as King Sebastian, the Duke of Avero, Lord Lodowick, Stukeley, and others met the Moor Muly Mahamet, Calipolis, their son, and others.

King Sebastian said, "Muly Mahamet, King of Barbary, we are well met, and welcome to our town of Tangier after this sudden shock and unlucky war.

"Welcome, brave Queen of Moors. Repose thee here, thou and thy noble son.

"And, soldiers all, repose you here in King Sebastian's town.

"Thus far in honor of thy name and aid, Lord Mahamet, we have adventured, to win for thee a kingdom, to win for ourselves fame, and to win performance of those promises that in thy faith and royalty thou have sworn to King Sebastian of Portugal."

The Moor Muly Mahamet had promised to make King Sebastian the overlord of Morocco if he would help him defeat Abdelmelec.

King Sebastian continued, "And thrive it so with thee as thou do mean, and mean thou so as thou do wish to thrive!"

In other words, may you thrive if you intend to keep your promises, and may you not thrive if you do not intend to keep your promises.

King Sebastian continued, "And if our Christ, for whom in chief we fight, hereby to enlarge the bounds of Christendom, will favor this war, and, as I do not doubt, send victory to land upon my helmet, then, brave Moor, I will promote thy kingly son, and with a crown of pearl and gold adorn thy temples and enrich thy head."

The Moor Muly Mahamet said, "Oh, brave Sebastian, noble King of Portugal, renowned and honored always may thou be, the conqueror over those who menace thee!

"May the hellish prince, grim Pluto, god of the Underworld, with his mace violently drive my soul down to hell, and with this soul let him drag down to hell this son of mine — the honor of my house — unless I perform religiously the holy vows that I have made to give to thee that which I have promised thee!

"And so that thy lords and captains may perceive that my mind is in this matter free from duplicity and is in this matter pure — as pure as is the water of the brook — my dearest son to thee I pledge: I hand him over to you.

"Receive him, lord, as a hostage to ensure I will keep my vow, for even my mind presages to myself that I shall behold Abdelmelec captured and then dragged like a slave along this running river shore: a spectacle to daunt the pride of those who climb aloft by force, and not by right."

Muly Mahamet's son said, "Nor can it otherwise befall the man — Abdelmelec — who keeps his seat and scepter all in fear, who wears his crown in the eye of all the world, a crown known to have been gotten by theft and not by inheritance.

"What title, then, has Abdelmelec here to bar our father or his progeny from the throne?

"Right royal King Sebastian, have no doubt or fear about helping us, an action agreeing with your wholesome Christian laws.

"Help, then, courageous lord, with hand and sword, to clear my father's way, whose obstacles are lawless men; and for this deed all of you shall be renowned, renowned and chronicled in books of fame, in books of fame and characters of brass, of brass — nay, of beaten gold.

"Fight, then, for fame, and you will find the Arabian Muly Mahamet here adventurous, bold, and full of rich reward."

Stukeley said, "Brave boy, how plain this princely mind in thee gives evidence of the height and honor of thy birth! I have well observed thy eagerness — which being offered by your majesty, no doubt the quarrel, opened by the mouth of this young prince impartially to us, may animate and hearten all the army to fight against the devil for Lord Mahamet."

King Sebastian said, "True, Stukeley; and so freshly to my mind has this young prince recalled the wrong done to his father that in good time I hope this honor's fire, kindled already with regard of right, bursts into open flames, and calls for wars, wars, wars to plant the true-succeeding prince.

"Lord Mahamet, I take thy noble son as a pledge of honor, and I shall treat him so.

"Lord Lodowick, and my good Lord of Avero, see that this young prince is conveyed safely to Mazagan and is there accompanied as befits him best.

"And to this war prepare you more and less,

"This rightful war, that Christians' God will bless."

CHAPTER 4

— Prologue —

The Presenter said, "Now hardened is this unfortunate heathen — non-Christian — prince, and strengthened by the arms of Portugal, this Moor Muly Mahamet, this murderer of his progeny, and war and weapons now, and blood and death, attend the counsels of this cursed king, and to a bloody banquet he invites the brave Sebastian and his noble peers."

Imagine this:

King Sebastian, Muly Mahamet, the Duke of Avero, and Stukeley attend a bloody feast featuring lots of blood, dead men's heads in dishes, and human bones. The Furies and Death also attend the bloody banquet.

The Presenter continued, "This peerless prince arrived in a fatal hour to lose his life and the lives of many vigorous men, courageous Portuguese, drawn by ambitious golden looks."

The golden looks were opportunities to achieve one's ambitions.

The Presenter continued, "Let fame of him no wrongful censure sound.

"Honor was the object of his thoughts, ambition was his ground."

— 4.1 —

Abdelmelec, Celybin, Zareo, and others met in the city of Alcazar. Celybin was Abdelmelec's chief scout. Zareo was one of Abdelmelec's military commanders. Abdelmelec's army was here at Alcazar.

Abdelmelec said, "Now tell me, Celybin: What is the enemy doing?"

Celybin said, "The enemy, dread lord, has left the town of Arzil with a thousand armed soldiers to guard his fleet of thirteen hundred sail.

"Mustering his men before the walls of Arzil, he found he had two thousand armed cavalry, fourteen thousand foot soldiers, three thousand laborers known as pioneers, and a thousand wagon drivers, besides an almost numberless number of drudges, negroes, slaves, and muleteers, stable-boys, laundresses, and courtesans, and fifteen hundred wagons full of stuff for noblemen brought up in delicate surroundings."

The Portuguese army was ill trained and ill managed. The noblemen had brought along with them way too many servants and way too many luxurious personal belongings. They were not used to military campaigns and battlefields.

Abdelmelec said, "Alas, good King Sebastian, thy foresight has been small, to come with women into Barbary, with laundresses, with baggage, and with trash, numbers unfit to multiply the soldiers of thy army."

Celybin said, "Their payment to the soldiers in the camp is surpassingly slow, and food is scarce, with the result that many faint and die."

Abdelmelec asked, "Where is he marching in all this haste?"

Celybin answered, "Some think he marches here with the intention of capturing this city of Alcazar."

"To Alcazar?" Abdelmelec said. "Unconstant chance!"

Lady Fortune is fickle, but for whom was King Sebastian's march unfortunate? For himself and his army because they were not prepared to fight a war, especially when heavily outnumbered? True. But it was also unfortunate for Abdelmelec because he was a good man whom history records as preferring not to fight.

Celybin said, "The brave and valiant King of Portugal quarters his power in four battalions, in the front of which, to welcome us, are placed thirty-six cannon.

"The first battalion, consisting of light-armed cavalry and the garrisons brought from Tangier, is led by Alvaro Peres de Tavero.

"Stukeley commands the left or middle battalion, which is composed of Italians and German horsemen. Stukeley is a warlike Englishman sent by the Pope, and he vainly calls himself the Marquis of Ireland.

"Alonso Aquilaz conducts the third battalion, which mostly consists of German soldiers.

"The fourth legion consists of none except Portuguese soldiers, of whom Lodevico Caesar has the chief command.

"In addition, there stand six thousand splendidly attired cavalry who are ready to fight where need requires.

"Thus I have told your royal majesty how King Sebastian is placed to brave us in the fight."

Abdelmelec asked, "But where's our nephew, the Moor Muly Mahamet?"

Celybin said, "He marches in the middle and is guarded on all sides by fully five hundred foot soldiers armed with arquebuses — firearms — and by six thousand useless soldiers armed with pikes."

Pikes are useful weapons against cavalry, but poorly trained soldiers would not be able to effectively use their pikes.

Zareo said, "Great sovereign, please hear me speak, and let Zareo's advice now prevail.

"While the time is still appropriate, and while these Christians dare to approach the battlefield with their warlike banners spread, let us quickly with all our forces meet them, and hem them in, so that not a man escape.

"That way, they will be careful another time how they touch the shore of Barbary."

Abdelmelec's army was much bigger than King Sebastian's army, and so his army could surround King Sebastian's army.

Using the royal plural, Abdelmelec said, "Zareo, hear our resolution.

"Thus our forces we will first dispose.

"Mahamet Seth, my brother, will have a thousand soldiers carrying firearms on horseback — all of them choice harguebuziers, and he will have ten thousand foot soldiers with spear and shield. These shall make up the right wing of the army.

"Zareo, you shall have in charge the left wing. You shall have two thousand light-armed horsemen and ten thousand cavalry.

"The main — center — battalion of foot soldiers carrying firearms, and twenty thousand horsemen in their troops, I myself will have in charge, surrounded by my trusty guard of janizaries, who guard me and are fortunate in war.

"And toward Arzil we will make our way.

"If, then, our enemy will balk our force and not fight, then in God's name let him — it will be the best thing for him.

"But if he aims at the walls of Alcazar, then beat him back with bullets as thick as hail and make him know and regret his recklessness — the recklessness of him who rashly seeks the ruin of this land."

— 4.2 —

King Sebastian, the Duke of Avero, and Stukeley talked together in the Portuguese camp north of the city of Alcazar. Others were present.

King Sebastian said, "Why, tell me, lords, why did you leave Portugal and cross the seas with us to Barbary? Was it to see the country and no more, or else to flee before you were attacked?

"I am ashamed to think that such as you, whose deeds have been renowned heretofore, should slack in such an act of consequence. We come to fight, and vow to die fighting, or else to win the thing for which we came.

"Because Abdelmelec, as if he were pitying us, sends us messages to counsel quietness, you stand stunned, and think it sound advice. As if our enemy would wish us any good.

"No, let him know we scorn his 'courtesy' and we will resist his forces whatsoever. Cast fear aside. I myself will lead the way and make a passage with my conquering sword, knee-deep in the blood of these accursed Moors; all they who love my honor, follow me.

"If you were as resolute as is your king, the walls of Alcazar would fall before your face, and all the force of this lord of Barbary — Abdelmelec — would be destroyed, even if it were ten times more than it is."

The Duke of Avero said, "So well do these words suit a kingly mouth that they are persuasive enough to make a coward fight. But when advice and prudent foresight are joined with such magnanimity, trophies of victory and kingly spoils inevitably adorn his crown, his kingdom, and his fame."

Bearing news, Christopher de Tavora, Don de Menysis, and Hercules entered the scene.

Hercules said, "We have seen upon the mountaintops a huge company of invading Moors, and they, my lord, will fall upon our heads as thick as winter's hail in a surprise attack.

"It is best, then, at once to take steps to avoid this gloomy storm. It is in vain to strive with such a stream."

The Moor Muly Mahamet entered the scene.

He said to King Sebastian, "Behold, thrice-noble lord, uncalled I come to counsel where necessity commands, and the honor of undoubted victory makes me exclaim upon this dastard flight.

"Why, King Sebastian, will thou now delay, and let so great a glory slip from thy hands?

"Let's say that you march to Larissa now. The forces of the foe have come so near that the foe will block the passage across the river, and so unexpectedly you will be forced to fight."

Larissa was a port town about a dozen miles away.

The Moor Muly Mahamet continued, "But know, king, and know, thrice-valiant lords, that a few blows will serve to achieve victory. I ask but only this, that with your army you march into the battlefield.

"For now all the opposing army is resolute to leave the traitor Abdelmelec helpless in the fight and fly to me as to their rightful prince.

"Some cavalry have led the way by already deserting the traitor, and they vow that their companions will do the same.

"The enemy army is full of tumult and of fear.

"So then as you have come to plant me in my throne, and to enlarge your fame in Africa, now — now or never — bravely execute your sound and honorable resolution, and end this war together with the life of Abdelmelec, who usurps the crown with tyranny."

King Sebastian said, "Captains, you hear the reasons of the King of Morocco, the Moor Muly Mahamet, which so effectually have pierced my ears that I am fully resolute to fight, and whoever refuses now to follow me, let him be forever accounted cowardly."

The Duke of Avero said, "May shame be the share of that man who flees when kings fight! I, the Duke of Avero, lay my life before your feet."

Stukeley said, "As for my part, lords, I cannot sell my blood dearer than in the company of kings."

Everyone exited except the Moor Muly Mahamet.

He said, "Now I have set these Portuguese to work cutting a path for me to the crown of Morocco. If they don't do that, then they will dig their graves with their weapons here.

"You bastards of the Night and Erebus, you fiends — you Furies — you hags that fight in beds of steel, range through this army with your iron whips, drive forward to this deed this Christian crew, and let me triumph in the tragedy, even if it is sealed and honored with the blood both of the King of Portugal and of the barbarous Moor Abdelmelec."

The Furies fight in beds of steel. In this poetic image, the steel is their armor, which they sleep in.

The Moor Muly Mahamet continued, "Ride, Nemesis, goddess of vengeance, ride in thy fiery cart, and sprinkle gore among these men of war, so that either party, eager for revenge, may honor thee with the sacrifice of death.

"And Nemesis, having bathed thy chariot-wheels in blood, descend and take to thy tormenting hell the mangled body of that traitor-king Abdelmelec, who scorns the power and force of the King of Portugal.

"Then let the earth discover to his ghost such tortures as usurpers feel below.

"Let him be racked in proud Ixion's wheel."

In the Land of the Dead, Ixion is bound on a flaming wheel that constantly spins.

The Moor Muly Mahamet continued, "Let him be tormented with Tantalus' endless thirst."

In the Land of the Dead, Tantalus stands in a stream of water with fruit-bearing branches above his head. Whenever he stoops to drink, the water level lowers and the stream dries up. Whenever he reaches for fruit to eat, the wind blows the branches just out of his reach. He is forever thirsty and hungry, and water and fruit are always just out of his possession.

The Moor Muly Mahamet continued, "Let him be prey to Tityus' greedy bird."

In the Land of the Dead, Tityus has been sentenced to lie chained on the ground as two vultures eternally dig into his body and eat his liver.

The Moor Muly Mahamet continued, "Let him be wearied with Sisyphus' immortal toil."

In the Land of the Dead, Sisyphus is punished to forever roll a boulder up a hill. Just as he reaches the top of the hill, he loses control of the boulder and it rolls back to the bottom of the hill again. Sisyphus can never accomplish his goal.

The Moor Muly Mahamet continued, "And lastly for revenge, for deep revenge, of which thou are goddess and deviser, damned let him be, damned, and condemned to bear all the torments, tortures, plagues, and pains of hell."

CHAPTER 5

— Prologue —

The Presenter said:

"May evil fall to him that so much evil thinks, and may evil befall this foul ambitious Moor Muly Mahamet, whose wily schemes with the smoothest flattery of speech have tied and tangled in a dangerous war the fierce and manly King of Portugal."

Lightning flashed and thunder sounded.

The Presenter continued:

"Now the heavens throw forth their lightning-flames and thunder over Africa's deadly battlefields. Blood will have blood; foul murder will not escape the whip of retribution."

Imagine this:

Fame, looking like an angel, hangs three crowns upon a tree.

The Presenter continued:

"At last Fame descends, as Iris did to finish fainting Dido's dying life."

Dido, the Queen of Carthage, fell in love with the Trojan Aeneas after Troy fell and the surviving Trojans led by Aeneas made an emergency landing in Carthage. The two had a love affair, and Dido was despondent after Aeneas left Carthage to fulfill his destiny of going to Italy and becoming an important ancestor of the Romans. She committed suicide by falling on her sword, and the goddess Juno sent another goddess, Iris, to cut her thread of life so she could enter the Land of the Dead.

The Presenter continued:

"The goddess Fame descends from her stately bower, and on the tree, like fruit newly ripe and ready to fall, she places the crowns of these unhappy kings, whom formerly she kept in the eye of all the world."

Imagine this:

A blazing star appears.

The Presenter continued:

"Now fiery stars and streaming comets blaze, which threaten the earth and princes of the same."

In this society, comets were regarded as ill omens.

Imagine this:

Fireworks appear in the sky.

The Presenter continued:

"Fire, fire whirls round about the axle of heaven, and from the foot of the northern constellation Cassiopeia, in a fatal hour, consumes these fatal crowns.

Imagine this:

One crown falls.

The Presenter continued:

"Down falls the diadem of the King of Portugal."

Imagine this:

The other crowns fall.

The Presenter continued:

"The crowns of Barbary and kingdoms fall."

The crowns of Barbary were those of the Moor Muly Mahamet and of Abdelmelec. The kingdoms were Barbary under the rule of the Moor Muly Mahamet and Barbary under the rule of Abdelmelec.

The Presenter continued:

"Alas, that kingdoms may not stand stable! And now approaching near the dismal day, the bloody day wherein the armies join in battle, Monday the fourth of August, in the year fifteen seventy-eight, the sun — the brightest planet in the highest heaven — shines wholly on the parched earth."

People in this society called the sun a planet.

The Presenter continued:

"The heathens, eagerly directed against their foe, begin the battle with much cannon-fire. The Christians with great noise of cannon-shot send angry military attacks against the enemy.

"Listen, and hear how war begins its song with dreadful clamors, noise, and the sound of trumpets."

— 5.1 —

The battle of Alcazar began. King Sebastian's Christian army formed a square formation because they were outnumbered. The Christian army fought well at the beginning and forced many soldiers of Abdelmelec's army, which had surrounded the Christians, to flee. Abdelmelec, who was ill, talked with Zareo, one of his military leaders. A train of attendants was present.

Sitting in his chair of state, Abdelmelec said, "Speak, Zareo, tell me all the news. Tell me what Fury wanders in our camp and has forced our Moors to turn their backs. Zareo, tell me what event predicted this ill, what ill compelled this despicable cowardice?"

Zareo said, "My lord, this is such chance as war provides; war is unpredictable. Such chances and misfortunes as these attend on Mars, the god of battle and of arms.

"My lord, after our fierce cannon-fire we sent our Moors into action with the smaller shot of their firearms, as thick and as quickly as hail follows hail, to charge the Portuguese army. But then the valiant duke, the devil of Avero, the death-dealing bane of Barbary, filled full of blood-lust, broke through the ranks, and with five hundred cavalry, all men-at-arms, eager and full of might, assaulted the middle wing, and put to flight eight thousand of our firearm-bearing foot-soldiers, and twenty thousand Moors with spear and shield, and by so doing the Duke of Avero won the honor of the day."

Abdelmelec said to himself, "Ah, Abdelmelec, do thou live to hear this bitter process of this first attempt in this battle?"

He then gave orders, "Labor, my lords, to renew our force of fainting Moors, and fight it out to the last.

"Bring me my horse, Zareo!"

He intended to mount his horse and go into battle to rally his troops.

His illness seized him, and he mourned, "Oh, the goal is lost! The goal is lost!

"Thou King of Portugal, thrice-happy chance it is for thee and thine that heaven abates my strength and calls me away.

"My sight fails; my soul, my feeble soul shall be released from prison on this earth. Farewell, vain world! For I have played my part."

Abdelmelec fell back into his chair of state and died.

As the fighting continued, Muly Mahamet Seth entered the scene. Because his older brother, Abdelmelec, had died, and he was next in line of succession, Seth was now the Sultan of Morocco and so had the title of Muly.

Seth looked at Abdelmelec, realized that he was dead, and said, "Brave Abdelmelec, thou thrice-noble lord! Not such a wound would be given to Barbary even if twenty armies of our men had been put to the sword, as Death, pale Death, with his fatal death-giving arrow has given to Barbary by taking you.

"Abdelmelec, my brother and my king, is dead, whom I might have revived with the good news that I bring."

Zareo said, "His honors and his insignias Abdelmelec has resigned to the world, and from a manly man, look, in the twinkling of an eye, he has become the senseless stock we see!"

Seth said, "You trusty soldiers of this warlike king, be counseled now by us and take this advice. Don't let Abdelmelec's death be reported in the camp, lest with the sudden sorrow of the news the entire army will be wholly discouraged and defeated.

"My Lord Zareo, thus I comfort you. Our Moors have bravely borne themselves in the fight and are likely to get the honor of the day, if anything may be gotten where such loss is present.

"Therefore, we will bring forward my noble brother, wearing this apparel he wore as he died, to the battlefield, and set him in his chair with cunning props to keep him upright, so that our soldiers of Morocco may behold their king, and think he is resting in his tent."

Zareo said, "Your advice is very shrewd and good."

Seth said, "Go, then, and see that it is speedily performed."

Zareo propped the body of Abdelmelec up in his chair.

Seth said to the corpse, "Brave lord, if Barbary recovers from this, thy soul with joy will sit and see the fight."

The fighting continued, and the Christians fled. On the battlefield, the Duke of Avero was slain.

On the battlefield, King Sebastian and Stukeley met and talked together.

King Sebastian said, "Don't thou, Stukeley, oh, Stukeley, see the great dishonor done to Christendom?

"Our cheerful attack thwarted in its springing — growing — hope.

"The brave and mighty prince, the Duke of Avero, slain in my sight. May joy now befall his ghost, for like a lion he bore himself in battle!

"Our lines of battle are now all disordered, and because of our cavalry's strange retreat our middle wing of foot-soldiers have been overwhelmed.

"Stukeley, alas, I see my error!

"False-hearted Moor Muly Mahamet, now, to my cost, I see thy treachery! I had been warned to beware a face so full of fraud and villainy."

King Sebastian exited, the battle continued, and two enemy soldiers attacked Stukeley.

In another part of the battlefield, the Moor Muly Mahamet and his young male servant — his page — were fleeing.

The Moor Muly Mahamet ordered, "Villain, get me a horse!"

Thinking that the Moor Muly Mahamet wanted a horse so he could return to the battle, the page said, "Oh, my lord, if you return, you die!"

Muly Mahamet said, "Villain, I say, give me a horse so I can flee — so I can cross the river, villain, and flee!"

His page exited.

The Moor Muly Mahamet said to himself, "Where shall I find some unfrequented place, some uncivilized land, where I may curse my fill, and I may curse my stars, my mother, my unlucky astrological planets, and my wet-nurse, and I may curse the fire, the air, the water, and the earth, and I may curse all the causes that have thus conspired in one, to nourish and preserve me so I can suffer this shame?"

He addressed the astrological star or planet — this society used the terms interchangeably — that had doomed him to suffer ill fortune:

"Thou that were predominate at my birth, thou fatal star, whatever planet thou be, spit out thy bad poison, and all the ill that fortune, fate, or heaven may foredoom a man."

He addressed others whom or that he blamed for his ill fortune:

"Thou malevolent wet-nurse, guilty of all, and thou mother of my life, who gave birth to me, cursed may thou be for bearing such a cursed son! Cursed be thy son with every curse thou have!

"You elements of which this clay consists — this mass of flesh, this cursed, crazed corpse — destroy, dissolve, disturb, and dissipate what water, fire, earth, and air congealed."

Amid the noise of battle, the page returned with a horse.

The page said, "Oh, my lord, these ruthless Moors pursue you at the heels, and come with full speed to put you to the sword!"

The Moor Muly Mahamet said, "A horse, a horse, villain, a horse! So that I may immediately cross the river and flee."

The page said, "Here is a horse, my lord, as swiftly paced as the flying horse Pegasus. Mount the horse, and save thyself by flight."

The Moor Muly Mahamet said, "I will mount the horse, but may I never pass the river until I am revenged upon thy soul, accursed Abdelmelec! If not on earth, then when we meet in hell. Before the grim judges Minos, Rhadamanth, and Aeacus, I will crave combat upon thy ghost and drag thee through the loathsome hellish pools of Lethe, Styx, and fiery Phlegethon."

He mounted the horse and exited.

Elsewhere on the battlefield, the enemy had wounded Stukeley. With him were Hercules and Jonas, who were angry at him for leading them to Morocco, where they had suffered this loss.

Hercules said, "Stand, traitor, stand, ambitious English-man, proud Stukeley, stand, and don't move before thou die. Thy eagerness to follow wrongful arms and leave our famous expedition that was intended by his Holiness for Ireland has here been foully betrayed and has tied us all to the ruthless fury of our heathen foe, for which, as we are sure to die, thou shall pay satisfaction with thy blood."

Stukeley said, "Go away, base villains! Do you reproach me with shame for the infamy of this injurious war when He Who is the Judge of right and wrong determines the outcomes of battle as pleases Him best?

"But since my stars foredoom me to this tragic end that I must perish by these barbarous Moors, whose weapons have made a passage for my soul to break out from the prison of my breast, then you proud malicious dogs of Italy, strike on — to the earth strike down this body, whose mounting, aspiring mind stoops to no feeble stroke."

Jonas asked, "Why do we allow this Englishman to live?"

Hercules and Jonas stabbed Stukeley.

Jonas continued, "Villain, bleed on; may thy blood run in channels and meet with the blood of those whom thou to death have done."

Hercules and Jonas exited.

Alone, Stukeley said, "Thus Stukeley, slain with many a deadly stab, dies in these desert fields of Africa."

He then addressed you, the readers of this book:

"Listen, friends; and with the story of my life let me deceive and not feel the torment of my death.

"In England's London, lordings, I was born on that brave bridge, the bar that thwarts the Thames River."

London Bridge had supports that partially dammed the river during the changing of the tides.

Stukeley continued, "My golden days, my younger careless years, were when I touched the height of Fortune's wheel, and lived in the affluence of wealth and ease and comfort.

"Thus I was in my country carried long aloft, but a discontented humor drove me from there to cross the seas to Ireland and then to Spain.

"In Spain I had welcome and right royal pay from Philip the Second, whom some call the Catholic King. There in Spain Tom Stukeley glittered all in gold, mounted upon his jennet — a Spanish horse — that was as white as snow, shining like the sun-god Phoebus Apollo in King Philip the Second's court.

"There, like a lord, famous Don Stukeley lived, for so they called me in the court of Spain, until, because of a blow I gave a bishop's manservant, a strife began to rise between his lord the bishop and me, for which we both were banished by the king.

"From thence to Rome rode Stukeley all ostentatiously, received with royal welcomes by the Pope. There Pope Gregory the Great graced me and made me Marquis of Ireland.

"My tale will be short because my remaining life is short.

"The coast of Italy and Rome I left. I was at the time made lieutenant general of those small forces that sailed for Ireland, and with my companies of soldiers I embarked at Ostia, which is located at the mouth of the Tiber River.

"I spread my sails, and with these men of war in a deadly hour we arrived at Lisbon.

"From thence to this — to this hard exigent — I, Stukeley, was driven to fight or else to die. I was dared to go to the battlefield — I who never could endure to hear Mars the god of war's drum but he must march.

"Ah, sweet Sebastian, had thou been well advised, thou might have managed arms successfully! But from our cradles we were all marked and destined to die in Africa here.

"Stukeley, the story of thy life has been told. Here breathe thy last, and bid thy friends farewell. And if thy country's kindness be so much, then let thy country kindly ring thy knell by ringing the bell.

"Now go and in that bed of honor die, where brave Sebastian's breathless corpse lies."

King Sebastian of Portugal had died before him.

Stukeley continued:

"Here ends Fortune's rule and bitter rage.

"Here ends Tom Stukeley's pilgrimage."

He died.

In another part of the battlefield, Muly Mahamet Seth and Zareo talked together. A train of attendants and some drummers and trumpeters were present. The Moroccans had won the battle with a general slaughter of the Christian soldiers.

Muly Mahamet Seth said, "Retreat has sounded throughout our military camp, and now our conquering Moors cease from battle's fury.

"Pay thanks to heaven with sacrificing fire, Alcazar, and you towns of Barbary."

Muly Mahamet Seth said to Abdelmelec's corpse, "Now have thou sat as if in a trance, and seen, to thy soul's joy and the honor of thy house, the trophies and the triumphs of thy men, great Abdelmelec; and the God of kings has made thy war successful because of the rightness of thy cause, as have the efforts of thy and His friends, whom death and fates have taken from thee."

He then said about Abdelmelec, "This was he who was the people's pride, and he who was cheerful sunshine to all his subjects! Now we will have him taken away from here, so that royally he may be buried and embalmed as is fitting."

He then asked, "Zareo, have you throughout the camp proclaimed what we previously ordered you to have proclaimed?"

Zareo said, "We have, my lord, and we have proposed rich rewards for them who find the body of the King of Portugal. For by those guards who had him in their charge we have learned and understand that he was done to death, and two prisoners, both of them Portuguese, have been set at large to search for and find the body of their royal king."

Muly Mahamet Seth said, "But you hear no news of the traitorous Moor who fled the field and sought to swim the ford?"

Zareo replied, "Not yet, my lord; but doubtless God will tell and with his finger will point out the place he haunts."

Muly Mahamet Seth said, "So let it rest, and on this earth we will bestow this kingly corpse of Abdelmelec until we provide further for his funeral rites."

Zareo took the crown from Abdelmelec's corpse and put it on Muly Mahamet Seth's head while saying, "From him to thee as true-succeeding prince, with all allegiance and with honor's signs, in the name of all thy people and thy land, we give this kingly crown and diadem."

Muly Mahamet Seth said, "We thank you all, and as my lawful right, with God's defense and yours, I will keep it."

Two Portuguese men carried in the body of King Sebastian.

The first Portuguese man said, "As your grace instructed us, right royal prince, we have surveyed the fields and sandy plains, and in the place where the corpses of Portuguese lords was the thickest, we found the corpse of the noble King of Portugal, wrapped in his colors — his royal banner — coldly on the earth, and done to death with many mortal wounds."

Muly Mahamet Seth said, "Look, here, my lords, this is the earth and clay of him who was a short time ago the mighty King of Portugal!"

He then said to the two Portuguese men, "There let him lie, and in return for finding his corpse, you are free to return from here to Christendom."

Two other men carried in the corpse of the Moor Muly Mahamet.

The first person said, "Long live the mighty King of Barbary!"

"Welcome, my friend," Muly Mahamet Seth said. "What body have thou there?"

The first person said, "This is the body of the ambitious enemy who squandered all this blood in Africa, whose malice sent so many souls to hell. I bring the body of the traitor Muly Mahamet, and as if he were thy slave I throw him at thy feet."

Muly Mahamet Seth said, "Zareo, give this man a rich reward.

"And thanked be the God of just revenge because He has given our foe into our hands — our foe who is beastly, unarmed, slavish, full of shame.

"But tell me, how did this traitor come to his end?"

The first person said, "Seeking to save his life by shameful flight, he mounted on a hotly spirited horse of Barbary, and as he attempted to cross the stream, his headstrong steed threw him from his seat into the stream, where, as he sank often because he lacked the skill of swimming, it was my chance alone to see him drowned.

"By the heels I dragged him out of the pool of water, and hither I have brought him thus defiled with mud."

The Moor Muly Mahamet was the third of three kings to die on this day of battle, and so the Battle of Alcazar is also known as the Battle of the Three Kings.

Muly Mahamet Seth said, "It was a death too good for such a damned wretch. But since our rage and rigor of revenge is forestalled by the violence of his end, we will do this: So that all the world may learn by him to avoid dragging kings into injurious war, we command that his skin be parted from his flesh and be stiffened and stuffed with straw in order to deter with fright those who see it from any such foul fact or bad attack. Take his corpse away!"

Some attendants carried away the corpse of the Moor Muly Mahamet.

Muly Mahamet Seth then said, "And now, my lords, here are my orders for this Christian king.

"My Lord Zareo, let it be your responsibility to see that the soldiers solemnly march, trailing their pikes and ensigns on the ground as a sign of respect, and with respect to perform the king's funeral rites."

APPENDIX A: ABOUT THE AUTHOR

It was a dark and stormy night. Suddenly a cry rang out, and on a hot summer night in 1954, Josephine, wife of Carl Bruce, gave birth to a boy — me. Unfortunately, this young married couple allowed Reuben Saturday, Josephine's brother, to name their first-born. Reuben, aka "The Joker," decided that Bruce was a nice name, so he decided to name me Bruce Bruce. I have gone by my middle name — David — ever since.

Being named Bruce David Bruce hasn't been all bad. Bank tellers remember me very quickly, so I don't often have to show an ID. It can be fun in charades, also. When I was a counselor as a teenager at Camp Echoing Hills in Warsaw, Ohio, a fellow counselor gave the signs for "sounds like" and "two words," then she pointed to a bruise on her leg twice. Bruise Bruise? Oh yeah, Bruce Bruce is the answer!

Uncle Reuben, by the way, gave me a haircut when I was in kindergarten. He cut my hair short and shaved a small bald spot on the back of my head. My mother wouldn't let me go to school until the bald spot grew out again.

Of all my brothers and sisters (six in all), I am the only transplant to Athens, Ohio. I was born in Newark, Ohio, and have lived all around Southeastern Ohio. However, I moved to Athens to go to Ohio University and have never left.

At Ohio U, I never could make up my mind whether to major in English or Philosophy, so I got a bachelor's degree with a double major in both areas, then I added a Master of Arts degree in English and a Master of Arts degree in Philosophy. Yes, I have my MAMA degree.

Currently, and for a long time to come (I eat fruits and veggies), I am spending my retirement writing books such as *Nadia Comaneci: Perfect 10*, *The Funniest People in Comedy*, *Homer's* Iliad: *A Retelling in Prose*, and *William Shakespeare's* Hamlet: *A Retelling in Prose*.

By the way, my sister Brenda Kennedy writes romances such as *A New Beginning* and *Shattered Dreams*.

APPENDIX B: SOME BOOKS BY DAVID BRUCE

Retellings of a Classic Work of Literature

Arden of Faversham*: A Retelling*

Ben Jonson's The Alchemist: *A Retelling*

Ben Jonson's The Arraignment, or Poetaster: *A Retelling*

Ben Jonson's Bartholomew Fair: *A Retelling*

Ben Jonson's The Case is Altered: *A Retelling*

Ben Jonson's Catiline's Conspiracy: *A Retelling*

Ben Jonson's The Devil is an Ass: *A Retelling*

Ben Jonson's Epicene: *A Retelling*

Ben Jonson's Every Man in His Humor: *A Retelling*

Ben Jonson's Every Man Out of His Humor: *A Retelling*

Ben Jonson's The Fountain of Self-Love, or Cynthia's Revels: *A Retelling*

Ben Jonson's The Magnetic Lady, or Humors Reconciled: *A Retelling*

Ben Jonson's The New Inn, or The Light Heart: *A Retelling*

Ben Jonson's Sejanus' Fall: *A Retelling*

Ben Jonson's The Staple of News: *A Retelling*

Ben Jonson's A Tale of a Tub: *A Retelling*

Ben Jonson's Volpone, or the Fox: *A Retelling*

Christopher Marlowe's Complete Plays: Retellings

Christopher Marlowe's Dido, Queen of Carthage: *A Retelling*

Christopher Marlowe's Doctor Faustus: *Retellings of the 1604 A-Text and of the 1616 B-Text*

Christopher Marlowe's Edward II: *A Retelling*

Christopher Marlowe's The Massacre at Paris: *A Retelling*

Christopher Marlowe's The Rich Jew of Malta: *A Retelling*

Christopher Marlowe's Tamburlaine, Parts 1 and 2: *Retellings*

Dante's Divine Comedy: *A Retelling in Prose*

Dante's Inferno: *A Retelling in Prose*

Dante's Purgatory: *A Retelling in Prose*

Dante's Paradise: *A Retelling in Prose*

The Famous Victories of Henry V: *A Retelling*

From the Iliad *to the* Odyssey: *A Retelling in Prose of Quintus of Smyrna's* Posthomerica

George Chapman, Ben Jonson, and John Marston's Eastward Ho! *A Retelling*

George Peele's The Arraignment of Paris: *A Retelling*

George Peele's The Battle of Alcazar: *A Retelling*

George Peele's David and Bathsheba, and the Tragedy of Absalom: *A Retelling*

George Peele's Edward I: *A Retelling*

George Peele's The Old Wives' Tale: *A Retelling*

George-a-Greene: *A Retelling*

The History of King Leir: *A Retelling*

Homer's Iliad: *A Retelling in Prose*

Homer's Odyssey: *A Retelling in Prose*

J.W. Gent.'s The Valiant Scot: *A Retelling*

Jason and the Argonauts: A Retelling in Prose of Apollonius of Rhodes' Argonautica

John Ford: Eight Plays Translated into Modern English

John Ford's The Broken Heart: *A Retelling*

John Ford's The Fancies, Chaste and Noble: *A Retelling*

John Ford's The Lady's Trial: *A Retelling*

John Ford's The Lover's Melancholy: *A Retelling*

John Ford's Love's Sacrifice: *A Retelling*

John Ford's Perkin Warbeck: *A Retelling*

John Ford's The Queen: *A Retelling*

John Ford's 'Tis Pity She's a Whore: *A Retelling*

John Lyly's Campaspe: *A Retelling*

John Lyly's Endymion, The Man in the Moon: *A Retelling*

John Lyly's Galatea: *A Retelling*

John Lyly's Love's Metamorphosis: *A Retelling*

John Lyly's Midas: *A Retelling*

John Lyly's Mother Bombie: *A Retelling*

John Lyly's Sappho and Phao: *A Retelling*

John Lyly's The Woman in the Moon: *A Retelling*

John Webster's The White Devil: *A Retelling*

King Edward III: *A Retelling*

Mankind: *A Medieval Morality Play* (A Retelling)

Margaret Cavendish's The Unnatural Tragedy: *A Retelling*

The Merry Devil of Edmonton: *A Retelling*

The Summoning of Everyman: *A Medieval Morality Play* (A Retelling)

Robert Greene's Friar Bacon and Friar Bungay: *A Retelling*

The Taming of a Shrew: *A Retelling*

Tarlton's Jests: A Retelling

Thomas Middleton's A Chaste Maid in Cheapside: *A Retelling*

Thomas Middleton's Women Beware Women: *A Retelling*

Thomas Middleton and Thomas Dekker's The Roaring Girl: *A Retelling*
Thomas Middleton and William Rowley's The Changeling: *A Retelling*
The Trojan War and Its Aftermath: Four Ancient Epic Poems
Virgil's Aeneid: *A Retelling in Prose*
William Shakespeare's 5 Late Romances: Retellings in Prose
William Shakespeare's 10 Histories: Retellings in Prose
William Shakespeare's 11 Tragedies: Retellings in Prose
William Shakespeare's 12 Comedies: Retellings in Prose
William Shakespeare's 38 Plays: Retellings in Prose
William Shakespeare's 1 Henry IV, aka Henry IV, Part 1: *A Retelling in Prose*
William Shakespeare's 2 Henry IV, aka Henry IV, Part 2: *A Retelling in Prose*
William Shakespeare's 1 Henry VI, aka Henry VI, Part 1: *A Retelling in Prose*
William Shakespeare's 2 Henry VI, aka Henry VI, Part 2: *A Retelling in Prose*
William Shakespeare's 3 Henry VI, aka Henry VI, Part 3: *A Retelling in Prose*
William Shakespeare's All's Well that Ends Well: *A Retelling in Prose*
William Shakespeare's Antony and Cleopatra: *A Retelling in Prose*
William Shakespeare's As You Like It: *A Retelling in Prose*
William Shakespeare's The Comedy of Errors: *A Retelling in Prose*
William Shakespeare's Coriolanus: *A Retelling in Prose*
William Shakespeare's Cymbeline: *A Retelling in Prose*
William Shakespeare's Hamlet: *A Retelling in Prose*
William Shakespeare's Henry V: *A Retelling in Prose*
William Shakespeare's Henry VIII: *A Retelling in Prose*
William Shakespeare's Julius Caesar: *A Retelling in Prose*
William Shakespeare's King John: *A Retelling in Prose*
William Shakespeare's King Lear: *A Retelling in Prose*
William Shakespeare's Love's Labor's Lost: *A Retelling in Prose*
William Shakespeare's Macbeth: *A Retelling in Prose*
William Shakespeare's Measure for Measure: *A Retelling in Prose*
William Shakespeare's The Merchant of Venice: *A Retelling in Prose*
William Shakespeare's The Merry Wives of Windsor: *A Retelling in Prose*
William Shakespeare's A Midsummer Night's Dream: *A Retelling in Prose*
William Shakespeare's Much Ado About Nothing: *A Retelling in Prose*
William Shakespeare's Othello: *A Retelling in Prose*
William Shakespeare's Pericles, Prince of Tyre: *A Retelling in Prose*
William Shakespeare's Richard II: *A Retelling in Prose*
William Shakespeare's Richard III: *A Retelling in Prose*
William Shakespeare's Romeo and Juliet: *A Retelling in Prose*
William Shakespeare's The Taming of the Shrew: *A Retelling in Prose*

William Shakespeare's The Tempest: *A Retelling in Prose*
William Shakespeare's Timon of Athens: *A Retelling in Prose*
William Shakespeare's Titus Andronicus: *A Retelling in Prose*
William Shakespeare's Troilus and Cressida: *A Retelling in Prose*
William Shakespeare's Twelfth Night: *A Retelling in Prose*
William Shakespeare's The Two Gentlemen of Verona: *A Retelling in Prose*
William Shakespeare's The Two Noble Kinsmen: *A Retelling in Prose*
William Shakespeare's The Winter's Tale: *A Retelling in Prose*